JULIUS JR.
STORY COLLECTION

Adapted by Courtney Carbone
from the scripts "Butterfly Dreams," "Rock Sock 3000,"
and "Pony Macaroni" by Katherine Sandford

A GOLDEN BOOK · NEW YORK

randomhouse.com/kids

ISBN 978-0-553-49859-2 (trade) – 978-0-553-49860-8 (ebook)

Printed in the United States of America

10 9 8 7 6 5 4 3 2 1

BUTTERFLY DREAMS

It was a bright, sunny day. Julius Jr. was wearing his Invento-vision hat and was looking for the perfect item to use in his next invention. "Eureka!" he exclaimed. He had found a shiny paper clip in the grass. He couldn't wait to turn it into something amazing!

Julius Jr. went inside The
Box to show Sheree, Ping, and
Clancy his awesome discovery.
"It looks like an ordinary
paper clip to me," Sheree said.
Julius Jr. smiled. "The best
inventors can make inventions
out of anything!"

Just then, Worry Bear burst into the room, laughing. "Something's tickling me!" he said, giggling. A little bug was crawling on his arm.

Julius Jr. quickly used the paper clip to make a mini staircase. The bug crawled down the little metal stairs. Soon the bug was off Worry Bear and on a table. "It's a caterpillar!" yelled Ping.

The caterpillar was trying to say something, but nobody could hear his tiny voice. Julius Jr. got his Amplificator out to help. The Amplificator made soft voices louder.

"My name is Sydney, and I want to be a butterfly!" the bug shouted.

"Why don't you make yourself a cocoon?" asked Sheree.

"I tried," Sydney replied, "but I can't."

"To the Invention Dimension!" Julius Jr. cried.

Julius Jr. was back in a flash.
"I present . . . the Cocoon-itron!" he
exclaimed. Julius Jr. had used items from the
clubhouse to make a cocoon-building invention.
"What could go wrong?" Clancy asked.
"Shall I start the list?" Worry Bear replied.

"Time to grow, Sydney!" exclaimed
Julius Jr., turning on the machine.
Everyone cheered.

"It's working!" Sheree said.

It *was* working—but perhaps too well!
In just seconds, Sydney had grown into a
gigantic bug and burst out of his cocoon!

Julius Jr. knew the clubhouse was no place for a
giant caterpillar. "To the Hall of Doors!" he shouted.
   Once inside, the friends stopped in front of a door
that looked like a ladybug.
   "You've come to the right place!" the door said.

Behind the door was a beautiful land called Bugswana.
"This is the perfect place for a giant caterpillar like me to
turn into a giant butterfly!" Sydney exclaimed.
"Pardon me, honey," said a voice. The group turned to see
two caterpillars sunbathing nearby. "You're not a caterpillar."

"You're brown with lots of legs," said the other caterpillar. "You're definitely a millipede."

Sydney looked down at his legs, then back at the two caterpillars. He did look different from them. He sadly realized that he would never become a butterfly.

Julius Jr. and his friends wanted to cheer Sydney up.

"Millipedes are the best," Ping told Sydney. "Look at all your feet!"

"Think of all the soccer balls you can kick!" said Clancy.

"And all the shine-erific shoes you can wear!" Sheree added.

Sydney thought for a moment. "I guess it is pretty great to be a millipede," he said. "It's just that I always wanted to be a butterfly so I can fly."

"Just because you're a millipede doesn't mean you can't fly," Julius Jr. told him. It was time for a new invention!

Julius Jr. and his friends hurried back
to the playroom. They used a ball of yarn
and an old umbrella to build giant wings for
Sydney. Then Julius Jr. turned his paper clip
into a Millipede Wing Flapper.

"Ready for takeoff!" Julius Jr. exclaimed.

"This is a dream come true!"
Sydney said as his friends climbed
on his back for a ride. "Thank you!"
Soon Sydney was flying high—just
like a real butterfly!

ROCK SOCK 3000

Julius Jr. was excited. He had just finished his latest invention, a giant slingshot called the Blastinator!

"It's ready to be tested," he announced. He looked around for something to launch.

"How about this?" Ping asked, holding up
Worry Bear's green sock monkey, Rocky.
"Eureka!" said Julius Jr. "That's it!"
Worry Bear was nervous. Rocky was his
best friend. Julius Jr. promised that Rocky
would be safe. He even put a little helmet on
Rocky's head to be sure.

Julius Jr. placed Rocky in the
Blastinator and began a countdown.
"Three . . . two . . . one . . ."
   "Blastoff!" yelled Clancy.
   There was a loud bang, and the sock
monkey was launched high into the
sky! Worry Bear covered his eyes.

A moment later, Ping caught Rocky in midair.
He was safe and sound.

"Rocky sure is cuddly," Ping said. "Can I hold
him for a while, Worry Bear?"

Worry Bear was nervous about sharing his toy,
but he agreed when Ping promised to be careful.

Suddenly, a delicious aroma floated
through the air. Sheree was baking in the
clubhouse! The friends slid down the slide
into The Box as fast as they could—and
landed on top of each other in the ball pit.

"You're gonna love my Shimmer Glimmer Cake!" Sheree announced. She handed out cupcakes to all her friends.

"Rocky, would you like a bite?" Worry Bear asked. He looked around for his sock monkey, but Rocky was missing! Ping couldn't remember where she had left him.

They searched the clubhouse, but no one could find Rocky.
Worry Bear missed his fuzzy friend. "What will I hug?" he cried.
"Don't worry," said Julius Jr. "There has to be something
huggable around here somewhere." He thought for a moment
and shouted, "To the Hall of Doors!"

Their first stop in the Hall of Doors was the giant hot-chocolate door. Inside were giant marshmallows!

"Too sticky," said Worry Bear. Rocky wasn't sticky.

Another door led to a room full of soft, fluffy clouds! Ping jumped in—*boing!*—and bounced right back out.

"Too bouncy," replied Worry Bear. Rocky wasn't bouncy.

The next room was filled with teddy bears!

"I don't think so," Worry Bear said. He wanted his stuffed *monkey*, not a stuffed *bear*.

Julius Jr. had one last idea.

"Hoozie-woozies!" he yelled, opening a round rainbow door. Inside was a colorful wonderland filled with adorable fluffballs!

But even the cuddly hoozie-woozies couldn't replace a friend like Rocky.

Julius Jr. wouldn't give up—he really wanted
to help his friend. He went into the Invention
Dimension and came out with his greatest
invention ever.

"*Ta-da!*" cried Julius Jr. "The Rock Sock 3000."
The super-smart sock-monkey robot was
programmed to comfort Worry Bear.

The new toy looked just like Rocky, but it wasn't the same. Worry Bear was still very sad. Then Ping had an idea!

"Why don't you tell it to find the real Rocky?" she asked.

"You're a genius!" said Julius Jr. He pressed a button on the robot's remote control.

"Initiating search," the robot said. It scanned the room with its sensors. "Target located."

The robot sped to the couch across the room. It reached deep into the cushions and pulled out . . . Rocky! The sock monkey had fallen behind the couch when Ping flew off the clubhouse slide.

"Rocky!" cried Worry Bear. He gave his old friend a big hug.
Julius Jr.'s invention had saved the day.
"The best inventions are the ones that help your friends!"
Julius Jr. said with a smile.

PONY MACARONI

Julius Jr. and his friends were spending a relaxing afternoon together in the clubhouse. All of a sudden, Ping saw something special across the room.

"Look!" said Ping. "A pony!"

"That's Clancy's hobbyhorse, Ping," Worry Bear told her. "It's not a real pony."

"Are you sure?" asked Ping as she ran across the room toward the pony.

Ping was right! Macaroni the toy
horse had turned into a real pony! Clancy
and his friends couldn't believe it.

Julius Jr., Sheree, Clancy, and Ping took turns riding Macaroni. She could do all kinds of neat tricks! Everyone was having a great time.

Everyone, that is, except Worry Bear. He was scared of Macaroni. When Worry Bear's friends dressed him up like a cowboy and finally convinced him to go for a ride, the pony ran away—straight to the Hall of Doors! Julius Jr. and his friends ran after her.

The friends found Macaroni hiding in the Sagebrush Farm corral. They needed to figure out what had scared her. It was time for one of Julius Jr.'s awesome inventions!

Julius Jr. took his Invento-vision goggles and added two horseshoes to make Pony-vision goggles.

"Eureka!" he cried. "Now we can see things the way Macaroni sees them!"

Julius Jr. looked at his friends through the goggles. There were smiley faces above Sheree and Ping. But Worry Bear had a worried face above him.

"I think I see the problem," Julius Jr. said. "Worry Bear, you're afraid of Macaroni, and she senses it."

"That means she'll feel better if Worry Bear isn't afraid!" said Ping.

Worry Bear took a deep breath. It was time for him to be brave. He slowly walked over to the pony and held out his hand.

"Hey there, Macaroni," he said, patting her gently. "There's nothing to be scared of."

Macaroni looked at him and smiled. She wanted to be friends, too.

Soon Worry Bear learned not to be scared of
Macaroni. He even took a turn riding her around
the farm! Everyone cheered.

Worry Bear was happy that he had been brave
and made a very special new friend. Yee-haw!